Y0-CBF-495

by Tony Norman

illustrated by
Paul Savage

Librarian Reviewer
Joanne Bongaarts
Educational Consultant
MS in Library Media Education, Minnesota State University, Mankato, MN
Teacher and Media Specialist with Edina Public Schools, MN, 1993–2000

Reading Consultant
Elizabeth Stedem
Educator/Consultant, Colorado Springs, CO
MA in Elementary Education, University of Denver, CO

 STONE ARCH BOOKS
Minneapolis   San Diego

First published in the United States in 2006
by Stone Arch Books,
151 Good Counsel Drive, P.O. Box 669,
Mankato, Minnesota 56002.

Originally published in Great Britain in 2005
by Badger Publishing Ltd.

Library of Congress Cataloging-in-Publication Data
Norman, Tony.
    Terror World / by Tony Norman; illustrated by Paul Savage.
    p. cm.
    "Keystone Books."
    Summary: Jimmy and Seb love playing the video games at Terror
World, but when the arcade's owner offers them a free trial of a new game,
they enter the real Terror World, where there seems to be no escape from the
vicious razor cats.
    ISBN-13: 978-1-59889-008-2 (hardcover)
    ISBN-10: 1-59889-008-5 (hardcover)
    [1. Video games—Fiction. 2. Arcades—Fiction. 3. Horror stories.]
I. Savage, Paul, 1971– ill. II. Title.
PZ7.N7862Ter 2006
[Fic]—dc22   2005026567

1 2 3 4 5 6 11 10 09 08 07 06

Printed in the United States of America

TABLE OF CONTENTS

Chapter 1

START THE GAME

Jimmy was being chased by ghosts through a dark cave.

Seb was lost in deep snow on a frozen planet.

Jimmy heard the ghosts scream and howl. Seb saw an army of aliens burst out of an icy sea.

Were they scared?

No! They were playing games at
Terror World!

Terror World was the best arcade
in town. The video screens glowed
brightly. Seb and Jimmy were lost
in the thrill of the games they were
playing. The ghosts and aliens seemed
real to them.

Then both their screens went dark.

"What's going on?" asked Jimmy.

"Don't know," said Seb.

"I turned your games off," said a voice from behind them.

The boys knew the man with the deep voice. He was the arcade owner. He had a bald head and big, dark eyes.

"Why did you do that?" asked Seb angrily.

"You're good at these games," said the man. "But are you ready for a real test of skill?"

Chapter 2

INTO TERROR WORLD

"What kind of test?" asked Jimmy.

"Yeah," added Seb. "What are you talking about?"

"The new Terror World video game," said the arcade owner. "You haven't seen it yet. Nobody has. You can both play it at the same time. Come and check it out."

When Seb and Jimmy saw the new game, they just stood and stared.

It had two cool motorcycles and a huge video screen.

"Neat," said Jimmy.

"Wow!" exclaimed Seb.

The arcade owner nodded.

"How much does it cost to play?" asked Seb.

"You can play for free," said the owner. "I want you to try it out for me. See what you think."

The boys looked at each other. This was too good to pass up.

Seb and Jimmy jumped on the motorcycles. The man pushed a button. The boys saw a bright flash of light and felt their bikes come to life. Then, in a rush of speed, they roared into the video screen.

Seb and Jimmy came out the other side.

They were in Terror World!

They raced around the streets of a dark city. High walls of red and black brick rose up to the sky. Fingers of green light glowed from every window. It was the kind of town bad dreams are made of.

Seb and Jimmy loved it.

The roads were smooth, like a race track. Their motorcycles zoomed along at incredible speeds.

And then, in a flash, it was over.

Jimmy and Seb were back in the arcade.

Chapter 3

RAZOR CAT

"Well?" asked the arcade owner.

"Terrific game!" said Seb.

"The best!" nodded Jimmy.

"There's an even better new game," said the man. "It's called Razor Cat, but . . ."

"But what?" asked Jimmy.

"I think it's a bit too scary for kids like you," the man said.

"No way," said Seb.

"Yeah, bring it on," said Jimmy.

"Well," said the man with an odd smile, "take a look at it first."

The new game had just one motorcycle, and they could see a wild cat moving on the screen. It seemed to be caged behind the glass.

"That's a razor cat," said the man. "Scared yet?"

"No," said Seb.

"It's only a game," said Jimmy.

"You've never played a game like this," said the man.

Seb and Jimmy smiled. They got on the motorcycle. "Let's do it," said Seb.

"You asked for it," said the arcade owner.

There was a bright flash of light and a rush of speed. The boys were back on the mean streets of Terror World. But they had lost their motorcycle.

"Where's our bike?" asked Jimmy.

"Don't know," said Seb with a shrug.

The two boys walked down the dark street.

"This game is boring," said Jimmy.

"Yeah, we can walk down a boring street at home," said Seb.

The boys laughed. Then they heard a sound that wiped the smiles from their faces.

"What was that?" asked Jimmy.

"I don't want to know," replied Seb.

The two friends made a run for it.

The roars grew louder. They could hear the scraping of long, sharp claws right behind them.

A razor cat was closing in fast.

Chapter 4

FACE THE FEAR

Jimmy and Seb ran for their lives.

"Quick, down here!" panted Seb.

They ran into an alley. Then they froze with fear.

They were in a dead end!

There was no way out. They stood against the wall at the end of the alley and turned to face the razor cat.

The razor cat looked just like the picture they had seen on the video screen. But this one was real, and it was twice as mean.

Tufts of purple hair stuck out of its dry, dusty body. It had blood-red eyes and long yellow fangs, like a vampire.

"It's a monster!" said Jimmy, in a shaky voice.

"Stay cool," said Seb, trying to think of a way out.

The razor cat gave a deep growl and moved closer.

Jimmy and Seb edged along the wall. They felt like rats in a trap. The cat could strike at any moment.

Then Seb tripped over something just as the razor cat lunged at him.

It missed!

Seb jumped to his feet and saw what he had tripped over.

"Quick, Jimmy," he said. "It's our motorcycle. Get on!"

Jimmy did what he was told.

Seb kick-started the bike. He tried to drive out of the alley, but there was no way past the razor cat.

The cat rose up on its back legs, razor sharp claws ready to strike.

Seb shut his eyes . . .

Chapter 5

ABOVE THE DANGER

LASH!

The razor cat's huge paw cut
through the air like a knife. It missed,
but the boys knew they were in danger.

Then their motorcycle took on a
life of its own. It gave a loud roar that
scared the razor cat.

The cat jumped back, and the bike
shot up into the air.

"Hold on tight!" shouted Seb.

The motorcycle flew out of the alley, leaving the razor cat alone and angry.

"We're free!" yelled Jimmy.

"All right!" said Seb. "Now, how do we get out of here?"

Chapter 6

GO FOR IT!

Seb and Jimmy flew high above the streets of Terror World. At first, it was fun. They felt they had won the game.

Then they heard the razor cat's roar.

Jimmy looked back. "He can fly! He's right behind us!"

The boys zoomed above a long, dark street and over a big park. What they saw below scared them even more.

The park was full of razor cats. They were staring at a huge movie screen.

"This can't be real," said Seb.

"Too weird," said Jimmy.

Their bike roared through the sky above the park.

When the razor cats heard the boys overhead, they roared with rage. The noise filled the air like thunder. The cats in the park were ready to fly up and join the razor cat from the alley, who was closing in fast.

"What now?" yelled Jimmy.

"Look at the screen," Seb shouted back. "It's the arcade!"

They could see the video games they loved to play.

"Let's try to get back!" said Seb.

Jimmy could feel the hot breath of the razor cat on his neck.

"Go for it!" he screamed.

Seb flew at the screen. The boys hit it at top speed. There was a flash of light and a loud bang.

Then a dark fog surrounded them.

Chapter 7

THE END?

Seb and Jimmy opened their eyes.

They were back in the arcade. The arcade owner was there with them.

"I need to talk to you," he said.

He seemed very nervous.

"No way," shouted Jimmy.

He and Seb ran for the exit.

Soon Seb and Jimmy were walking through a park they knew well. They were both still in shock.

"This place seems quiet," said Seb.

"I like it that way," smiled Jimmy.

They were happy to feel safe again.

Then they heard a sound that made their skin crawl.

"That's just the wind, right?" Seb asked Jimmy. "It can't be a razor cat, can it?"

"I dare you to turn around and look," said Jimmy.

"Run for your life!" yelled Seb.

As Jimmy ran after Seb, he yelled, "But the game's over!"

Or was it?

ABOUT THE AUTHOR

Tony Norman is a children's writer and poet from the South Coast of England. He started writing at school, where he dreamed up stories about scary places like Terror World.

Tony's hobbies include singing and playing guitar. Loyal fans include the frogs, toads, and fish in his garden pond!

ABOUT THE ILLUSTRATOR

Paul Savage works in a design studio, drawing pictures for advertising. He says illustrating books is "the best job." He's always been interested in illustrating books, and he loves reading. Paul also enjoys playing sports and running.

He lives in England with his wife and daughter, Amelia.

GLOSSARY

alley (AL-ee)—a narrow passageway between buildings

arcade (ar-KADE)—a place with machines for amusement, such as pinball and video games

fang (FAYNG)—a long, pointed tooth

lash (LASH)—to whip back and forth

pant (PANT)—to breathe quickly and loudly

shock (SHOK)—the state of being upset because of a sudden, violent event

tuft (TUHFT)—a bunch of hair

vampire (VAM-pire)—a dead person from folktales and horror stories who rises from the grave to feed on human blood

DISCUSSION QUESTIONS

1. Does the arcade owner know that the Razor Cat game is dangerous? If so, why does he ask Jimmy and Seb to play?

2. After Jimmy and Seb make it out of the Razor Cat game, the arcade owner says he needs to talk to them. But Jimmy and Seb take off without listening to him. What did the arcade owner want to tell the boys?

3. At the end of the story, Jimmy and Seb think they're being chased by a razor cat. How could the cat have escaped from inside the game?

WRITING PROMPTS

1. Razor cats aren't like common cats. They have purple hair and yellow fangs, and they can fly. Choose another type of common animal. Describe what that animal might look like if it were a dangerous beast inside a video game.

2. When the story ends, we do not know if a razor cat is really behind Jimmy and Seb. Write what happens after they start running.

3. If you were going to create your own video game, what would it be like? Would it have aliens or wild animals? Would it involve motorcycles or racecars? Describe it.

ALSO BY TONY NORMAN

Nervous
1-59889-018-2

It's time for the Dream Stars competition. The cool kids think their band Elite is a sure win. But what happens when a couple of nerds decide to start up their own band called Nervous?

OTHER BOOKS IN THIS SET

Something Evil
by David Orme
1-59889-017-4

A big city is built on the shore of Dark Lake, which can only mean one thing — big trouble. Discover who, or what, is causing the people living near Dark Lake to disappear.

Splitzaroni
by K. I. White
1-59889-014-X

Naseem always runs for cover when his mom returns with the groceries. When she comes back with a weird new plant, it seems she might have gone too far.

INTERNET SITES

Do you want to know more about subjects related to this book? Or are you interested in learning about other topics? Then check out FactHound, a fun, easy way to find Internet sites.

Our investigative staff has already sniffed out great sites for you!

Here's how to use FactHound:

1. Visit *www.facthound.com*

2. Select your grade level.

3. To learn more about subjects related to this book, type in the book's ISBN number: **1598890085**.

4. Click the **Fetch It** button.

FactHound will fetch the best Internet sites for you!